GW00467580

The
House of Death

Christian Brancati

Horror

Title: The House of Death

Author: Christian Brancati

Cover: MiblArt

ISBN: 9798376842713

First Edition

I dedicate this book to my Mom who is not afraid of anything.

*Inspired
by a true
personal story*

Summary

01

Spring Break

The crystal clear sea of the West Coast was gorgeous that morning. John loved surfing on the big waves of California. They were about two meters tall and were scary, but the boy with his sky blue surfboard rode the waves with mastery, for him it was like walking barefoot on the ground. The white Santa Monica Beach was full of people having fun swimming and sunbathing on lounge chairs or stretched out on beach towels. The nearby kiosks sold drinks and people danced under a hot sun. Near the beach there were cute hotels, they had been built right by the sea. The lifeguard from the white booth oversaw the entire beach. From a distance, you could see boys and children having fun on the Ferris wheel, the Santa Monica Ferris Wheel located on the most famous pier in California. The numerous palm trees embraced the beach giving it warmth and harmony.

"The sea is gorgeous!" John shouted, then began to look into the depths of the ocean.

John was 24 years old, born and raised in the city of Los Angeles. He loved the sea, he was five feet ten inches tall, weighed 159 pounds and had an athletic physique. His eyes were green, his hair was ash blonde and he wore it with a tuft upward. He had a small nose and thin lips. He did not like to wear a beard and shaved it off every morning. He was wearing a light blue swimsuit with a white vertical line drawn above it.

"Come on! Don't always sit on that surfboard!" said Janine, a girl with long, wavy black hair. She had brown eyes, a small and straight nose, pronounced lips and a slim physique. She was five feet six inches tall and wearing a two-piece purple swimsuit. Her skin was fair and she often got sunburns.

Janine splashed water on him, then started riding the waves with a purple surfboard. John followed her with the sky blue board. The girl raced through the waves, it was difficult for him to keep up with her. He almost managed to catch her, when a giant three-meter high wave overwhelmed him and made him do several somersaults underwater.

"Did you want to catch me? But someone caught you!" she said laughing.

"But stop it!" John countered with a smile.

The two teenagers got out of the water and lay in the sun on that beautiful white sandy beach. They were tired, they had worked hard practicing their favorite sport. A common passion that bound them deeply.

After a few minutes, their friends arrived.

"Hey bro, you did a great job with those waves!" said Robin, a tall, muscular African American boy. He had curly hair, blue eyes, and a small nose. He wore a short beard and an orange short-legged suit. He wore neon-colored flip-flops.

"Let's enjoy these days!" interrupted Rooney, a slightly overweight boy who loves cheeseburgers. He was short, with red hair and green eyes, a potato-shaped nose, and was wearing a white underwear suit. His beard was thick and well-groomed, and he pulled a chocolate snack out of his pocket and started eating it without remorse.

"Where are the girls?" asked Janine.

"Barbara is at the bar getting a drink, while Lizzy should be arriving soon" replied Robin.

"So, what are we doing for this Spring Break?" asked Rooney with his mouth full.

"Cancun?" proposed Janine.

"Caribbean?" proposed John.

"Ibiza?" Barbara interjected just arrived with a drink, full of ice and fruit, in her hand. She was a blonde girl, the typical girl who loves to dance and have fun who forgets about commitments and all the important things to do. She was thin, with two chestnut-colored eyes that captured attention, her nose was upturned, and she was wearing a red two-piece Levi's suit.

"Are you crazy? It's on the other side of the planet!" retorted Lizzy, just arrived. She was a voluptuous girl, not thin but not fat either. She wore dark red glasses, had short purple hair, a nose ring and wore a green two-piece suit.

"I have no preference, the important thing is to have fun! Especially eat in quantity! What can I offer you Lizzy?" said Rooney, but the girl did not reply.

The boys laughed together. It was that time of year, Spring Break. For a week, they were free from exams and university studies. A whole week of partying, from March 15th to 22nd. For them, 2020 had reserved great surprises. They all studied at the same university, the famous Skyfall University of California. They studied different subjects and had an age between 23-25 years. John studied ancient languages, Janine medicine, Rooney art, Barbara philosophy, Robin engineering and finally Lizzy computer science. They had met during a year-end party of the Los Angeles Venice High School four years ago, right on that beach where they were lying in the sun.

"Why don't you go to Kansas City?" interjected a young man with green hair, a muscular physique and a white underwear suit.

"And what do you know, Mike?" replied John.

"I went there a few years ago. We have the California sea just a stone's throw away. There's no point in traveling thousands of km to Cancun. It's better to enjoy a different place, the fun is everywhere. I don't know if I explain myself" said Mike with a twinkle in his eye to the girls and then left.

"He's not entirely wrong!" said Lizzy.

"I'm in!" added Rooney.

"Okay, but we girls will be in one room and you guys in the other!" said Barbara.

"Agreed!" said the boys.

"I'll book the room, in a luxurious hotel called Kansas City Universal! I know a way to book it at a rock bottom price!" said Robin confidently.

"Oh, yeah? Then I'll take care of it for us. We girls will stay in the nicest suite in the hotel!" retorted Lizzy.

"We have little time to book and leave!" John pointed out.

"Relax brother, pack your bags. We're leaving for Kansas City tomorrow!" said Robin excitedly.

"I'll take care of the plane, this time we'll fly with the Royal Air of America. Make sure to pay me tomorrow, I'm not a millionaire. The tickets are a fortune!" said Lizzy and everyone else started laughing.

"So, it's settled! An impromptu trip is just what we needed!" said Janine and John felt a strong warmth inside him when he saw her smile.

The boys left the beach, each of them set out on the way back. They had half a day to pack their bags, book the trip and then leave. John left the most beautiful beach in California, picked up his gray backpack and walked among the trees that created a path away from the beach. These were ten-meter-high palm trees, his home was at the end of the road and not far from Santa Monica Beach. It was surrounded by greenery, it seemed like being in a jungle. The house was made of pure chestnut wood, all around there were palm trees, plants, shrubs and flowers. John's parents were great naturalists and botanists who worked for the most prestigious universities in California. They had made many discoveries near their home. From the Papaya they managed to extract an enzyme called Papasi by them, it was able to detoxify the carcinogens contained in smoked meat. They had therefore created their own diet and even John was forced to follow it without being able to rebel.

"Now we're going to eat roasted chicken with coconut sauce!" said his mother Marie when John entered the kitchen.

She was a woman in her sixties who looked youthful. She was slightly plump, smart, esteemed and respected throughout the state. She had un-dyed brown hair, green eyes, a small nose and plump lips. She wore a long dress down to her feet with short sleeves of purple color and black low shoes.

"Why do I have to put up with all this!" John complained.

"Oh, come on! For dessert there's a fruit platter with whipped cream!" said his father Jerry.

He was older than his wife, wore glasses and had a slender physique. His eyes were blue and he had a few gray hairs on his head. He was also respected by everyone in the country. He wore a yellow t-shirt, white shorts and slippers.

"Sure, but made with goat's milk!" Marie retorted.

"I knew it!" John cursed.

The wooden house had a black sloping roof made with eco-friendly tiles. A series of solar panels was installed above the tiles, the energy of the Sun providing them with electric power for light, appliances, heating and air conditioning. Clean energy with the production of minimal amounts of toxic waste.

"Go get the fruit!" John's mother told him.

The boy went outside and started picking fruit from the trees that surrounded the house: bananas, figs, dates, papayas, mangoes, and even passion fruit. He also took some turmeric and red chili from their vegetable garden.

"It's crazy hot. I need to get moving on packing, we're leaving tomorrow!" John said with excitement.

He entered the house through a red triangular shaped door. The floor was dark wood, while the walls were a lighter and sweeter brown. The light bulbs hung from the ceiling attached to chandeliers shaped like ropes. The entrance was spacious and on the left was a coat hanger on the wall. On the right, a staircase led to the first floor of the house. After a short corridor on the left, you entered the kitchen. It was big, with a table with seven chairs, a deluxe fridge, a refined stovetop and a marble sink on the left side of the room. On the right was a beige couch in front of a large window that let in light and separated the room from the green that surrounded the home.

John gave the fruit to his mother and sat down at the table. He started browsing the photos of Kansas City on social media. He loved discovering new places and couldn't wait to leave.

"Tomorrow I'm leaving with my friends!" John said. Marie and Jerry were taken aback.

"You've gone crazy! Without even telling us!" said Marie.

"And with what money?" Jerry asked.

"Don't worry, it will only be for a week. I had saved money for the occasion, and we'll split the expenses among ourselves" replied John.

"You're just giving me headaches! Let's eat now!" said Marie with agitation.

"Where are you going?" asked Jerry with curiosity.

"To Kansas City! With a direct flight!" replied John.

Mom felt faint. "Don't take the plane!"

She had always been afraid of flying and had only been on a plane twice in her life. They had to put her to sleep with a benzodiazepine, but she still had bad memories of that trip, which, according to her husband, was calm.

"Calm down Marie, they're going to the city. They'll be fine!" said Jerry as he opened a bottle of liquor he made, the "Black Mangus" made with 3/4 mango and 1/4 alcohol.

After finishing dinner, John realized it was already 3 PM. He went up the stairs and went to his room. It was spacious, with posters on the walls depicting his heroes, from music to movies, to manga characters. The bed in the room was big, with emerald-colored cotton sheets, in front of the bed was a 25-inch TV and on the left was a gray desk in the shape of an "L" with a black latest-generation laptop. There was a small closet on the right wall with all his clothes and attached to a small white bookshelf full of books.

"Now comes the annoying part" muttered John.

He pulled out a medium-sized blue suitcase from under the bed. He put it on the bed and opened it. It was full of compartments and could hold many things despite its size.

"So, we'll be gone for seven days. So, I have to take seven underwear and seven pairs of socks" he took them and put them in the bag.

"What's the weather like? Cold or hot? Is it raining?" He checked the weather on his phone and saw that there would be fluctuations between 20 and 35 degrees.

"It will be hot, but better to bring something heavy and also an umbrella" he thought.

He put six shirts, three sweatshirts, eight pants, and a tracksuit in the suitcase. Then he took the slippers, soap, pine-scented shower gel, toothbrush, and xylitol toothpaste. He folded the clothes precisely and managed to get everything he needed for the trip in the suitcase. He put an umbrella, texts, and other things in the gray backpack.

"Well done! Now it's time for a shower!" he said contentedly.

John was thinking about his trip with Janine while taking a shower, wondering what he would eat without having to stick to his mother's strict diet. He wanted to visit the Kansas City Zoo where there were all kinds of animals, see the elephants, monkeys, polar bears, and especially take the Sky Safari, a cable car that allowed you to see the animals from above. He was curious about visiting the Arrowhead Stadium football stadium where the Kansas City Chiefs team played, seeing Caravaggio and Van Gogh's paintings at the Nelson-Atkins Museum, and trying the delicious dishes in the city's best restaurants.

"I hope I can see all these places with Janine" John said with his hands in his soapy hair.

After washing and drying, he put on an orange short-sleeved shirt and black pants. He lay down on the bed and picked up his latest smartphone.

"Tomorrow, departure at 5:40 am at bus stop number 9. The plane will leave at 8:30 am from Los Angeles airport. We will arrive at 12 with Spratz American Airlines' direct flight. $110 for the ticket, the return trip is included. Be on time!" wrote Lizzy in the WhatsApp group called "Fun Trip."

"Well done!" - Rooney.

"Great!" - John.

"What's the hotel like?" - Janine.

"Is there a pool?" - Barbara.

"Yes, you'll be stunned!" - Lizzy.

"Did you book Robin?" - Rooney.

"I used a new site, Bookstarg! It will be a great surprise!" - Robin.

"Did you book a room at the Kansas City Universal hotel like I told you to? With breakfast and lunch included?" - Lizzy.

"Relax, baby. Think about buying chips, popcorn, nachos, and anything else you want. It will be an unforgettable vacation!" - Robin.

"I can't wait" - John.

"Me too!" - Janine.

John blushed for a moment, the girl made him uncomfortable. He loved being with her more than anyone else. The idea of the vacation had put him in a good mood. Before he knew it, it was 8 pm. He went downstairs to have dinner with his parents, who were muttering to each other about plants and strange things. John was used to it and often didn't pay attention to their words.

"Eat, son, a vegetable minestrone with a pinch of turmeric and chili pepper. It will be the last decent meal you will have before you leave!" said Marie, upset.

"Or maybe this will be the last bad meal before departure" John thought.

"And then there's the roasted pork with 'Jerry's sauce' made of top-quality vegetables! It's your favorite dish!" Jerry said, putting the dish in front of John.

"I'll be gone for a week, not a year!" John said and his parents laughed.

"Eat and fortify yourself. Say goodbye to Janine for me tomorrow" said Marie.

"Why?" John asked.

"Just because" his mother whistled.

John didn't pay attention to her and ate everything that was given to him. As soon as he finished eating, he went to the bathroom to brush his teeth. Marie and John tidied up the kitchen, then went to bed in their bedroom facing John's room. It was a spacious room with a bed that had a wooden frame and a water mattress, two pillows with goat wool, and a small LCD plasma television placed in front of the bed. To the right there was a plum-colored bedside table and to the left a two-door green cabinet near a small window.

"Dear, I'm worried about John. What if something happens to him?" said Marie in bed.

"Have faith in him, he knows how to take care of himself and others" Jerry replied.

John returned to the room and put on a blue pajama set composed of a short-sleeved shirt and shorts. He lay down on the bed and turned on the smart TV. Thanks to the internet, he used the Netfiction portal to enjoy episodes of his favorite TV series The Demon Tamer, where a young warrior fought against demons inside the Coliseum. After watching two episodes, it was already late. He said goodnight to his friends in the group and went to sleep.

"Kansas City, we're arriving!" he mumbled, half asleep.

02

Depart

"It's the final countdown!" The ringtone of the smartphone woke John up from a deep sleep. It was just 5:10 in the morning and John was feeling groggy. He went to the bathroom, took a quick shower, washed his face and teeth. He went back to his room, put on a blue hoodie, dark green pants, and a pair of blue McGonagall sports shoes, which were very comfortable. It was cold outside, 6°C. Fortunately, he had already packed his bags and everything he needed. John put on his backpack and picked up his suitcase with his right hand.

"Have a good trip!" his parents said as they walked into the room.

"Thank you!" John replied.

"I prepared something for the trip, go downstairs to the kitchen" said Marie.

The three of them went downstairs to the kitchen, John saw a brown package and took it, then put it in his backpack. There was money on the table.

"500 dollars? That's a lot!" John was amazed.

"You earned it, have a good trip!" Jerry said.

John hugged his parents affectionately, put the money in his brown wallet, and then put on his gray jacket. He then left the house and Jerry and Marie waved goodbye from a distance. The boy walked down the street among the trees and after a few minutes he reached St. James Street, the road that would take him to the bus stop number 9. Along the way, he looked at the sea on the horizon. He already knew he would miss it, as he saw a mirage of happy dolphins jumping in the distance.

"Hey brother, it took you long enough!" Robin said under the bus stop. The boy was wearing a white wool hat, a red jacket, and a gray jean. He was wearing black sneakers, as usual. He had a small black trolley and an orange bag with him.

"Come on, we're still in time!" Rooney said with joy. He was calm, wearing a white bomber jacket, a green beanie, black pants with gray stripes, and dark loafers. He had two bags full of stuff, probably food.

"Where are the girls?" John asked.

"Here we are!" the three girls yelled in unison from a distance. They were all hooded and wearing gloves. Janine had a purple jacket, Barbara had a pink one, and Lizzy had a green one.

The hat and gloves were the same color as the jacket. They were wearing elegant and famous brand shoes. All three had huge luggage. "They brought too many things" John thought.

The boys grouped all under bus stop number 9, well indicated by the sign with a blue bus on a gray sidewalk and palm-lined.

"It's coming!" Robin shouted, spotting the bus from a distance.

The boys signaled the blue bus driver to stop. He was a fifty-year-old, plump and fair-skinned man. He wore a green driver's uniform.

"Tickets?" the driver asked politely.

"Yes, 6 tickets please" Lizzy replied.

Everyone paid their 7.5$ ticket and then took their seat in the central part of the bus. Robin was next to Rooney, John next to Lizzy, and finally Barbara next to Janine. The bus was running at great speed, and the boys looked out the window at the sea and beaches of Los Angeles. In no time, the bus brought them to the entrance of the airport with the LAX sign posted at the entrance gate. They got off in front of the main entrance, took their luggage, and headed for the station to take the direct flight to Kansas City 355. Lizzy took charge of the group, and the boys followed her.

"Our flight is at gate 25!" Lizzy shouted, having read the number on a monitor.

They started running as fast as they could with all that luggage among the crowd of people filling the entire airport. It was easy to get lost, there were similar hallways. In addition, it had numerous bars and shops to buy souvenirs. Arriving at their flight gate, they saw the stewardesses in red uniforms calling passengers on flight 355.

"Tickets and documents in hand, please!" the stewardesses said.

Lizzy gave the ticket to each of them, and the boys lined up one behind the other and passed the check-in without any problems. Their luggage was taken by the stewardesses and placed in the hold of the plane. The boys entered the landing strip where there were the planes. They were huge and white. They boarded a small purple bus that took them right near their plane. It was smaller than the others and had a smaller number of passengers. It was all gray, and the boys were surprised when they saw it. For a moment they thought of the worst.

"Will it take us to our destination?" Robin joked.

"Stop it!" Lizzy complained.

"Let's board" John said. "My mom would never step on it" he thought.

The boys climbed a metal ladder that allowed them to reach the plane door at a height of five meters from the ground. The flight captain, a young man, greeted them along with the flight attendants who had first taken their luggage and carried it to the hold. The plane had thirty seats arranged in two rows with three seats per row. The seats were made of velvet and were red in color. The three boys sat close to the three girls on the same right row of seats. John was near the window, then there was Rooney in the center, and finally Robin. Behind them were Janine, Barbara, and Lizzy in a similar manner.

"Fasten your seat belts, we're taking off" said the pilot over the PA system.

"Guys, I'm scared!" said Rooney.

"Come on, we'll have fun!" said Robin.

The plane took off without any problems. Each of them decided to pass the time in a different way, Barbara started flipping through a fashion magazine and kept trying to involve Janine, but she was only blowing in the wind, so the girl spent her time looking at the clouds and the view from the window. Rooney ate every kind of junk food, Lizzy worked on the computer, Robin listened to music with headphones so big it looked like he had a helmet on, and finally, John was reading a newly bought book called "The Rebirth of Evil."

"It's full of mysteries this novel" John whispered.

"Do you want anything to eat?" an attendant interrupted.

"No, thank you" John replied.

Robin took off his headphones and looked at John reading.

"Have you decided to talk to her?" asked Robin.

"Who?" said John.

"Don't play dumb, brother. With Janine" whispered Robin.

John felt uncomfortable and didn't dare turn around. "You're crazy, she's right behind me."

"Relax, she didn't hear" said Robin, facing backwards towards Janine. "It's your chance, brother. I'll try with Barbara. I've always had a weakness for her."

After those words, Robin went back to listening to music, John went back to reading.

The trip was peaceful, without turbulence and interruptions. When ten minutes remained before landing, the pilot said to stay calm. From the window, the landing runways of the airport in the shape of three concentric circles could be seen. The plane landed softly on platform number 7. The boys got off the plane one by one and went inside a black, large, and spacious bus. After eight minutes, they arrived at the entrance to Kansas City airport.

"We need to take the suitcases" Janine said.

"You're right!" John said.

"This way!" Lizzy, who always knew where to go, said.

It was a nice airport, big and full of bars and cafes. The kids got a coffee at Starbucks to recover from the trip. John got one with a hazelnut flavor and liked it a lot. They went to a spacious room and took their luggage from the conveyor belt, then sat on gray metal chairs not far from the airport exit.

"It's 2 in the afternoon!" Barbara said.

"How is that possible? Weren't we supposed to arrive at 12?" Rooney asked.

"My mistake, sorry. There's a different time zone, we're two hours ahead of California" Lizzy explained.

"Let's go eat somewhere in town!" Robin proposed.

"First we need to go to the hotel!" John said.

"By the way, what room are you in?" Lizzy asked.

"206" Robin answered.

"And us?" Barbara asked.

"26" Lizzy replied.

"That's strange, weren't we supposed to be close?" John asked.

"You're right! On the website it says there are rooms from number 1 to 50!" Lizzy said, showing the phone to the kids.

"Are you sure you made the reservation, right?" Rooney asked, giving Robin a suspicious look.

"Yes! Look!" the boy said and showed the reservation on his smartphone to the friends.

Lizzy had a shocked expression, the others didn't understand what had happened.

"You're an incapable! I knew I should have done it myself!" Lizzy shouted at Robin.

"What happened?" Rooney asked, separating the two.

"He booked a namesake hotel, it's not the same hotel! It's a different Kansas City Universal!" Lizzy replied.

"Where is it?" Janine asked worriedly.

"I'll check online now" John said.

He opened Maps and typed in the address of the hotel. When Lizzy saw the location of the hotel that Robin had booked, she was shocked.

"I don't believe it! You booked a hotel on the left side of the Kansas River! So, the hotel is in the state of Kansas! Our hotel, on the other hand, is in Missouri!" Lizzy said.

"I don't understand anything!" Barbara said while scratching her head.

"Maybe they're close. How far away are they from each other?" Janine asked.

"Unfortunately, no, they're 20 kilometers apart. Kansas City is a city in the state of Missouri, but there is also another city of the same name that belongs to the state of Kansas. In fact, the two cities create a single metropolitan area. Additionally, there is a bridge that crosses the Kansas River and separates the two cities that have the same name!" John said.

"Guys it's not my fault! Anyone could have made a mistake!" Robin said.

"But how can you say that? Now the vacation is ruined!" Lizzy said, going berserk.

"Calm down!" John shouted.

"Come on, calm down. Let's look for a place where we can all stay together" Janine proposed.

"Is that possible?" Rooney asked.

"Yes. Fortunately, the reservation can be canceled without losing money. And thankfully I didn't spend my own money! I'll solve the matter in 5 minutes. Give me your phone, Robin" Lizzy said resignedly.

"But I wanted to take a bath in the pool!" Barbara complained.

"You used a fake website, says the fake. Your hotel isn't even half of ours. It doesn't even have the same number of stars. Plus, you would have had to pay double what we did" Lizzy said.

"Come on, what does it matter? Let's find a different one, just being together is enough" John said, calming everyone down.

Suddenly, a little man approached them stealthily.

"Excuse me, young people, I overheard your argument and I'm saddened by it. My name is Edgar Mitchell and I own a house that I'll gladly rent to you at a discounted price!" the man said, introducing himself. He took off his hat and made a bow.

The boys looked at each other with great amazement. It was an elderly man, short, with gray hair in a crew cut, a parrot nose with a large black wart, dull black eyes, some missing teeth and a sparse beard. He wore a light blue vest over a shabby black sweater, brown pants and worn black shoes. On his head he had a well-groomed light brown beret.

"How much do you want, old man?" Robin asked without thinking.

"Wait, Robin!" John called out.

"400 dollars a week" replied the elderly man.

"Great! We save a lot!" said Rooney.

"Actually, yes, it's less than 1/3 of what we would have had to pay" added Lizzy.

"Is there a pool?" asked Barbara.

"I'm sorry my dear, there's everything but the pool" replied the man. Barbara resigned herself.

"Where is the house located?" asked John.

"Not far from here. It's in the middle of nature, you'll like it!" replied the old man.

"Let us think about it" said Robin.

The boys walked away for a few minutes and started talking among themselves.

"Right now we don't have many alternatives, even if we wanted to book a room we would pay triple at any hotel" Lizzy pointed out.

"I don't like this old man!" Robin replied.

"Neither do I, but if it's the only alternative to stay all together, I'm in" said John.

"OK" added Janine.

The others agreed as well. They went to the house owner and the old man smiled at them.

"We accept!" said Robin confidently.

"Well, well! Follow me!" the old man exclaimed with a clap.

The boys left the airport and saw the man get into a small green pickup truck used for hay transportation. There were only two front seats, one for the driver and one for the passenger.

"Get in the back!" the man ordered, leaning out the window.

"Is he crazy?" complained Lizzy.

"Dammit...let's get in, we have no choice" convinced Robin.

The boys got on board one by one and sat on the golden hay. It was soft. The old man started the truck and the truck started on their unknown destination.

03

The House

The truck was racing at high speed, the boys could barely sit and hold their luggage that was swaying back and forth. They crossed a bridge overshadowed by metal structures that intertwined and formed a X. As soon as they left the city of Kansas City, the old man took I-35, the number 35 interstate, towards Wichita. It was a wide road with four lanes where cars raced at high speed. On the sides of the road there were green meadows with rich vegetation. Now they were in the state of Kansas, they had left Missouri and their vacation in Kansas City behind.

"Where are we heading?" asked Rooney.

"Definitely not to Topeka, my GPS shows we're moving away from there" replied Lizzy.

"It's going to be a nature vacation!" John marveled, looking around. There were meadows, lakes and rivers. The boy also saw marmots drinking. The trees were in bloom, spring had arrived.

"I like it. We can go on hikes, visit cow or pig farms, watch stars and eat marshmallows around a campfire!" said Janine.

"What time is it?" asked Robin, he was tired.

"Almost 3" replied Barbara, who could barely hold herself on a bale of hay.

"Let's eat something!" said Rooney and took out bags of chips from his bag.

"Good! Tastes like pizza!" said Lizzy. She took chips on the fly and made a single bite.

"There are also those with curry and green pepper!" Robin noted in amazement.

The truck passed under a small tunnel carved into a gray rock mountain and abandoned the main road. The more he drove the road, the more he ventured into the green and the path became asphalt-free. At a fork he turned right, the road became rocky and full of stones. In the distance, you could see new, larger rivers and lakes than the previous ones. After about five kilometers, he arrived on a dirt road surrounded by pines, sequoias and tall oaks.

"It seems like we're going higher and higher" Robin noted in perplexity.

"You're right, strange" replied Barbara.

The truck began to climb up a steep road that led up a mountain. With little effort, it managed to cover it all, then stopped for a moment. The old man accelerated with force and the truck continued its ascent along the dirt road that surrounded the mountain rich in vegetation. The Sun seemed to get lost among the shrubs.

"I have a feeling that we will never forget this vacation!" said John.

The truck continued to climb, there was no one on the road. It was all deserted, no man or animal in sight. They arrived almost at the top of the mountain and saw the entrance of a small town with a shabby gray sign on which was written Marcoons.

"Marcoons? Where have we ended up?" said Robin with great perplexity.

It was a small town with about thirty small brick houses, some newer and others older with dangerous roofs. The houses were all close together, they seemed to be fused together. The boys passed a white church, it was old but beautiful. A large circular rose window let light into the building. The truck crossed the small town undisturbed and continued to climb up. The eyes of the passersby looked at them with a fixed and inquiring gaze.

"What do these guys want?" asked Robin.

"They have clothes from farmers old by a hundred years. I feel like I'm in the Far West!" chuckled John.

"I need a relaxing bath, this trip really tired me!" complained Barbara.

"I think I'll do it later too" said Robin mockingly.

They passed through a black gate three meters tall and finally the old man stopped the truck. They found themselves in the garden of a giant house. The outside had a small red barn on the right where in addition to the hay there were chickens hatching eggs. The garden was well-kept, it was green and full of flowers. There were daisies, roses, primroses and geraniums of various colors.

"This garden is beautiful!" said Janine as she got off the truck along with the others. "Yes, you're right. Those white flowers are adorable" noted Barbara.

"White?" said John.

The house had a Victorian style and was enormous. It had a series of rectangular windows on the ground floor, on the first floor there were small white marble balconies that stood out from the entire gray structure. The black roof tiles formed a particular pattern, the windows on the top floor had small gabled roofs. There was a very tall smoking chimney, reaching eight meters in height, while the roof reached six meters. On a cornice you could see the statue of a small monkey positioned near a window, on the left side of the house you could see a small tower, part of the structure, with three windows that ended at the top with a cone-shaped form and on the tip you could see the statue of a small elephant with a shiny appearance. On the back you could see the presence of a veranda supported by Ionic style columns. The entrance was preceded by three steps, it had a black door with an arched shape. On the door was engraved a strange symbol similar to an A that could be seen from a distance.

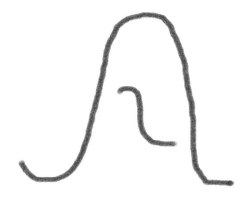

"This house is very strange" said Lizzy.

"I see it well kept, it's huge!" Barbara countered.

"I want the room on the top floor!" Janine demanded, sweetly.

"Please, follow me this way" the owner interrupted, just getting off the truck.

The kids followed him in front of the entrance, the man took out of his pocket a silver key with a round head, a long stem and a series of grooves and engravings. He opened the door. With a creaking sound, the house welcomed the new guests. Once inside, the owner greeted them from outside.

"Don't you come in?" Barbara asked.

"No, no, I have to do. Enjoy your stay, make yourself at home" he said with a frightened tone.

"Does he want the money now?" Robin asked.

"Don't worry, I'll see you tomorrow" the man said, then climbed into the truck and left.

"What a strange guy, I've never seen a landlord who didn't take the rent and didn't cross the door of his own house" Rooney said, amazed.

"He must have been scared of those skulls at the entrance!" said Lizzy.

"Really? Where are they? I didn't notice!" exclaimed John.

"There were three skulls, one next to the other" explained Janine.

"They must be fake, let's forget about them. Now let's start settling into this place. It's a nice house but too old for my taste. There's even mold and it's full of cobwebs in the corners of the ceiling" said Robin.

"And what do you expect, the owner barely sets foot in this house! He's never cleaned!" pointed out Rooney.

As soon as they crossed the threshold, they entered a spacious and rectangular room with pink flesh-colored walls. Under their feet was a brown carpet with strange swirls drawn on it, on the ceiling was an antique crystal chandelier that charmed them with its charm. Barbara pressed the switch and turned it on. The light illuminated the room, the kids left their luggage in the entrance and began walking straight to a green door, the only one they could open. Robin opened it and they entered a new room. On the left was a coat rack, the kids took off their jackets, hats and gloves.

"It's nice here, finally" John pleased himself.

"It must be the warmth of the fireplace, it's just like the one at my house" said Barbara.

They had entered a large living room with brown walls and paintings hanging on the walls. They depicted hunting scenes, birds, ducks, foxes and deer. In the center was a rectangular wooden table with ten well-finished and cared-for chairs. Here too, there was a beautiful crystal chandelier on the ceiling. On the left were hazel-colored sofas where the kids sat down to rest. The fireplace was in the upper left corner of the room, the wood was burning and warming the whole house. On the right were three windows that allowed you to see the outside garden.

"No, I can't believe it!" said Lizzy.

"What?" asked Rooney.

"No signal!" replied Lizzy. The kids all took out their phones and saw that there was no signal.

"No line, no internet. Will there be a TV?" asked Robin.

"I really don't think so" replied Barbara.

"There's a phone on that wall" John noticed.

It was a typical black disk phone from the late 1800s with white numbers and a black receiver resting on it.

"Order me a pizza then!" Robin said sarcastically.

"What hunger. Let's go to town to buy something, I bet the meat is great here" suggested Rooney.

"Okay. What time will it be?" said Lizzy.

"6 in the afternoon, we have to hurry before sunset" Robin advised.

The boys put on their coats and left the main door.

"Where is the key?" Barbara asked.

"The owner didn't give it to us" Janine answered.

"Just lock it, who's going to come to this strange place. There's no point in locking this strange door" Robin suggested.

Meanwhile, John had noticed the skulls placed on the ground near the ventilation grates in the basement. There were three of them, of different sizes, and they followed a decreasing size from right to left. The barn with the chickens had been closed, John walked away from the dwelling with his friends and saw that the monkey statue on the roof had disappeared.

"How strange, maybe I just imagined it" he said to himself.

The boys passed through the black gate that isolated the dwelling from the rest of the town. The road was mountainous and steep, and around them there were many leafless bushes. It was cold, they were 200 meters high compared to the town of Marcoons.

"Ooh!" Rooney was about to slip on a rock.

"Be careful brother! Then you roll down to the town and make a strike!" Robin said, and everyone else laughed.

They were well hooded, with gloves and scarves. None of them had expected there to be such cold and isolated from the world.

"Guys, say what you want, tomorrow I'm going home. Call that farmer and get me to Kansas City!" Barbara said while walking blindly.

"Come on, we just arrived. I'll keep you company!" Robin said, taking her hand and the girl blushed.

Janine was leading the group, followed by Lizzy, then Barbara and Robin, behind John and finally Rooney, who couldn't get used to the steep and difficult road to travel.

04

Marcoons

They arrived at the mountain village which was four hundred meters high. The houses seemed ancient and not belonging to our time. They were made of bricks and were next to each other. The brown and gray color of those homes was unsettling. They were two-story, with rectangular glass windows and a single entrance. They seemed to be falling on them, the slope of the mountain had forced the citizens to adapt to the mountain. John was the first to set foot on the white stones of the town floor. They were all the same and arranged in an orderly and precise manner. In about an hour sunset would arrive and the boys had to hurry if they wanted to stock up. The main street they were walking on was between two rows of houses, it was narrow and dilapidated. They arrived in a square with a dolphin-shaped fountain in the center. Numerous alleys radiated from this square; the boys had reached the heart of the town. On the right was a white stone church with a black cross on the top. The bell tower was seven meters high and on the bells were small singing angel statues. On the left and in front of them was a portico under which were shops, wineries, taverns. About twenty people animated that place, and as soon as they saw the boys, they were stunned.

"Please this way! Come and drink good wine!" said a stout host with a brown cowboy hat on his head. He had thick black mustaches, brown eyes and a buffalo carved on his leather vest. He wore a long black pants and brown boots.

"Come and buy my prime meat!" said the butcher with a white apron.

Some children were playing tag with ropes, they almost caught Rooney.

"Will it be a carnival party? Do they have cowboy outfits?" asked Rooney.

"I like it!" exclaimed Barbara.

"I don't think so. They have old clothes, look at those women over there. Their robes are long and end with a wavy skirt. The men have hats on their heads, leather vests and pants that seem all the same" explained John.

"That old man next to the pole has a black eye patch and a pistol in his waist" warned Robin.

"The elderly ladies have more sober attire and wear a headband" noticed Lizzy.

"It may be true what you say, but I smell beans. Let's eat something!" said Rooney and the others nodded.

The guys entered the tavern called "The Black Buffalo". The doors were typical of those of a saloon. Inside there were round tables with a few wooden chairs around them, on the walls there were buffalo, deer, wild boar and other stuffed hunting animals. Behind the bar, an old man with a black vest was cleaning some tin glasses.

"I didn't think I'd find the Old West Pub in this strange place!" Rooney boasted.

"You're welcome!" said a pretty blonde girl with green eyes. She was five foot six, wore a blue Victorian style dress that reached her feet. She had two braids that reached her belly. She was joyful and smiled often, wearing black shoes.

"What would you like to eat?" the girl asked.

"For me, a double cheeseburger with bacon and barbecue sauce" Rooney answered quickly.

"I don't understand, what would that be?" the girl asked with a surprised look.

"Ah ah, my dear, let me handle it. My daughter doesn't understand foreigners sometimes. Welcome to the Black Buffalo, you can eat slices of high-quality buffalo meat with delicious potatoes and beans. Beer and wine at will for the friends of the Skull Mansion" the host said.

"How does he know?" Janine asked.

"The town is small, we're about fifty people. Old Edgar is used to inviting people to his home. The dinner we're serving now is all offered by him!" the host replied.

"That crazy old man?" Robin was amazed.

"Can we eat as much as we want?" Rooney asked.

"Of course, it's all for you!" the girl replied, gracefully and kindly serving the dishes at the table.

It was tender and juicy meat, they ate it with great enthusiasm along with roasted potatoes and brown beans. The utensils they used were wooden and the beer mugs were tin. The guys ate with joy, while the host's daughter, at that moment, felt sad and went away in tears.

"I have to do something, this time I will!" she promised herself, inside the kitchen.

"Judith don't dare disobey your father!" said a man with white hair, a long nose and a black monk dress.

"Nicolas, but how can we stand by and do nothing?" Judith asked.

"It's not up to you to decide! We're in God's hands!" the priest scolded her.

Meanwhile, the boys had finished eating and it had become dark. Some men outside the tavern were lighting lamps that had oil lamps inside. Inside the establishment, candles were lit.

"This place looks like a movie scene" said Rooney.

"I told you I wanted to leave!" Barbara yelled.

"Calm down, we're on vacation. Relax. Think about what's happening in China and other countries because of the virus. There are also many cases in the United States. It's a tragedy, we will always remember 2020" said Lizzy.

"Thrum" the sound of thunder was heard.

The old owner entered from the door and looked at them with inquiring eyes.

"Here's where you were! Did you like the dinner?" he asked the kids.

"It's delicious meat!" replied Rooney.

"It's time to go home! A storm is coming, come with me!" the owner exhorted them.

The boys looked at each other and from their resigned look it was understood that they were forced to go back to that house.

"Thank you for dinner. Give my regards to your daughter" John said to the host.

"It will be done! Good stay" the host replied.

The boys left all together and Judith saw them leaving and felt sorry.

"I will pray for you!" Judith said with her hands crossed. "You will be able to defeat the House of Death!"

John and the others followed the old man into a narrow alley under the inquiring eyes of the townsfolk. They seemed to want to say something, but they could not speak. John had understood, sometimes a look says more than a thousand words. There was something strange about that little village, it was all well-made and organized. Everything clean, without anything out of place.

"There are horses" said Janine.

"Of course, noble steeds" replied the owner.

Between the houses a barn appeared with black horses, which seemed restless due to their presence. After passing them, they arrived at the old owner's pickup truck. They all climbed aboard and retraced the dirt road through the green.

"Look at a monkey!" said Rooney, seeing a chimpanzee among the trees.

"Maybe! I would have loved to visit the Kansas City zoo!" John complained.

"You'll dream of it, brother. We all need a good sleep, I'm exhausted" yawned Robin.

"Carry on my waywaaard son! For there'll be peace when you are done! Lay your weary head to rest. Don't you cry no more!" sang Rooney.

They returned to their dwelling, got out of the truck, and saw many candles lit in the garden. They arrived at the front door and the owner opened the door with the silver key.

"Could you give us a copy of the house key?" John asked.

"Oh, don't worry, you'll be safe tonight" the old man said in a hoarse voice.

"Don't worry about it, let's go inside" said Robin.

They all went in and then closed the door. The owner disappeared into nothing in a short time. As soon as they entered, they turned on the switch and the bright chandelier lit up the dining room. They sat at that table and took off their jackets. Outside there was a very strong wind that showed no signs of stopping.

"It's always warm in this house. I really need to put on my pajamas" Barbara said.

"But where are our bags?" asked Lizzy.

"I don't see them anywhere" replied Rooney.

"Has that old man taken them?" Robin got angry.

"I don't think so" said John, looking outside the windows with the black curtains.

"Excuse me, but didn't we leave our bags in a pink room?" asked Janine.

The six of them looked around and noticed something strange.

"I remember that when we entered, the first room had pink walls" said Robin.

"It's true! It's gone!" Lizzy realized.

"The windows were on the left wall, now they are in front of the front door" said John.

"Is this a joke? Are we on TV?" Barbara asked with a scared laugh.

"Let's go over there" said John, pointing to a door on the right wall.

The boys walked through it and found themselves in front of a wooden staircase. To the right was a long hallway with a series of doors, to the left a strange green door separated the house from the outside.

"Open it" said Robin.

John opened it, he found himself on the porch. It was large and spacious, there were old chairs and the floor was wooden. The garden seemed peaceful. John leaned out from the railing and noticed the three skulls that were about three feet from the door. In front of him was the barn with the chickens and then he noticed something even stranger. The white flowers seemed to have their own light and in a spot in front of the smallest skull there was an empty space devoid of white flowers. He closed the door and noticed that his friends were no longer there.

"Where are you?" asked John with fear.

"We're upstairs! Come up!" replied Robin.

John started climbing a stone staircase with agitation, it was made of three ramps that seemed endless. He was inside the tower of the house. At the second ramp he stopped and arrived at a yellow door. He opened it. At the same time the front door and the one that led to the porch disappeared into nothingness.

05

Let's play

John faced a long corridor with eight cream-colored doors. The walls were white and in front of him was a blue door with the word "Bathroom" written on it.

"This house is fantastic!" exclaimed Rooney as he just came out of the first room on the right. He was ravenously eating a cheese-flavored chips bag.

"But where did you find them?" asked John.

"I don't know, my room is full of food. Come in!" said Rooney.

The room had red walls, a small bed with blue sheets, and a table filled with chips, snacks, cola, and fizzy drinks. It had been set up for someone as if they were expected.

"There's also a TV with my favorite show, Supernatural!" said Rooney. The boy lounged on the bed and started watching the thirty-inch screen on the wall while eating popcorn and drinking orange juice at will.

John was perplexed, he went out and opened the first door on the left. He noticed it was empty, there was only a black rocking chair and some bags containing unknown objects.

So, he knocked on the second door on the left.

"Come in, brother" said Robin.

"What are you doing?" asked John.

"I'm playing this new car video game!" replied Robin.

"But where does this television with this latest generation console come from?" asked John.

"No! I was about to win!" said Robin.

John realized that his friend had been enchanted by the video game. It was his passion, once he had won a state tournament and brought home ten thousand dollars. The room had blue walls, a bed with green blankets, a mini-fridge filled with chilled beers, and a bedside table with a green spherical lamp.

"Where are the girls?" asked John.

"In front of me is Barbara, I have no idea where the others are" replied Robin, glued to the TV screen. He didn't even take his eyes off for a moment.

John went out and knocked on the second door on the right. After five minutes, Barbara came to open it. She had all her hair in front of her eyes and curlers in her hair.

"Who are you?" asked Barbara.

"I'm John" replied.

"Oh, sorry John, with this hair I can't see. I'm getting ready. This room is a dream. It's full of fragrances and makeup, the walls are pink. The bed is comfortable and full of cushions like I like it. I'll be ready in twenty minutes" said Barbara, then closed the door in his face.

"This one's crazy!" complained John.

The boy walked on the green floor of the hallway and knocked on the third door on the left.

"Who is it?" asked Janine with a timid voice.

"It's John" he replied.

"Eehm... I can't open now. Sorry, John, really" said Janine, wearing only lingerie and a bra.

John was embarrassed, but he regained his composure when he heard strange screams coming from behind him. He knocked on the third door on the right and Lizzy opened the door accompanied by an infernal noise.

"Turn down the volume, Lizzy!" John yelled.

"The volume doesn't go down! It's pure rock! Come in and sing with me!" replied Lizzy.

The room was all purple and had a computer with three screens, a hi-fi system, and a chandelier made of electric wires hanging from the ceiling. The bed was round-shaped and green.

"It's too loud for me. Better to go away!" said John.

"Oh, Rock you baby! Rock on now!" the girl sang.

John was stunned, these rooms were strange and his friends seemed under the spell of a spell. He opened the fourth door on the left and was amazed to see all his things. His black laptop was placed on a corner desk in front of him, on the right there was a bed with grey blankets, the walls were cream-colored, and there was an antique-style bookshelf with all his books.

"Who put all these things here? The owner? This is strange, that old man is hiding a secret. It's like he was spying on us and knows everything about us" he spoke to himself.

He looked around more closely and saw his luggage with his clothes inside, he closed the door and changed. He wore a blue jumpsuit with a gray shirt underneath. The room was warm, from his room through two windows he could see the garden. It was dark, he saw on his cell phone that it was almost midnight. All this story had upset him. Meanwhile, the chandelier on the ceiling swayed like a pendulum.

"Knock, knock".

"Who is it?" John asked.

"It's me" Janine replied.

John opened the door, the girl had combed her hair. Now they were long and straight, she wore a pink sweater and a blue jean.

"Do I disturb you?" Janine asked.

"No, come in" John replied.

"You know, I'm afraid to be alone. This house is strange, the rooms are beautiful and have everything I want, but that little village of Marcoons scared me. The inhabitants were strange, they wore strange clothes and looked at us with strange eyes" said Janine.

"It's the same thing I thought, someone is spying on us. We have to leave tomorrow morning, this place is hiding something" said John.

"Don't scare me! Try to catch me instead!" The girl gave him a small push and ran out of the door. She ran back and forth along that immense corridor.

"That's strange, I remember that this corridor was narrower now" John thought.

"Come on, catch me!" said Janine, she seemed to be three hundred meters away from him.

Meanwhile, while the two of them chased each other, Robin sneaked quietly into Barbara's room, Rooney walked towards the yellow door that led to the lower floor, and Lizzy went to the bathroom.

John was running as fast as he could, but Janine managed to surpass him. They seemed like two participants in an endless marathon. Only the boy had realized that the space of the house had changed, the rooms were further away from each other. He couldn't grab Janine's hand. When he arrived at the exit door, he stopped for a moment and lost sight of the girl. John started running, passed by the first door on the left and saw for a moment the figure of a girl with black hair gathered in two braids, a black dress in the '800 style with pleats, swaying on a rocking chair. It was just a moment, but it seemed eternal.

"Is that Janine?" he thought.

He wasn't sure of what he had seen, he was running at high speed and he couldn't see that mysterious figure clearly. He thought it was Janine and went back. He felt a mix of fear and surprise, opened the door wider and entered. To his great surprise, he noticed that the room was empty. There were only blue envelopes with strange objects that he dared not touch. The walls of the room were white, there were no windows. An old chandelier descended from above, the light bulb was about to blow. His eyes fell on the black rocking chair that, despite being empty, continued to rock. John approached the rocking chair and stopped it with his hands. He sat down and started to rock.

"I must have imagined it" he thought.

Meanwhile, Lizzy was alone in the bathroom. It was huge, as soon as you entered that blue-walled environment you faced a giant round bathtub. There was a hot tub, on the left there were three bathrooms for men and on the right for women. It was all neat and fragrant. In front of the entrance and behind the tub there were four sinks with big, shiny mirrors.

"What a nice way to relax" said Lizzy.

The girl had her eyes closed and was immersed in a lavender-scented foam, the hot tub was caressing her skin. Only her head was out of the tub, the quiet had put her in a good mood. She gently washed her body, then put shampoo on her head and started massaging her scalp. She used a showerhead to wash her hair. After all that rock, she had decided to relax.

"I have to say, this house is not too bad. I was wrong to talk badly about it."

At that moment, there was a scratching noise on the glass.

"Who's there?" Lizzy asked with fear. She looked around and saw no one.

"Let's play. Let's plaaay!" said a child's voice insistently.

"It must have been someone's TV" she said softly.

Lizzy removed the foam with the water jet coming from the showerhead, turned her eyes to the mirror and looked at herself with a satisfied look. At that moment, her image disappeared, the image of a young girl appeared in the four mirrors. It was the same girl that John had seen, but Lizzy did not know. She had two black eyes that cried blood, a broken nose, thin lips, and a ruined dress that revealed a battered and putrid body.

"Ahh! Help!" Lizzy shouted and at that moment the bathroom door disappeared. The girl panicked even more. With the showerhead, she sprayed water against the glass and the image of the girl disappeared.

"It's just a dream. I must get out of here. It's not real!" said Lizzy.

A brutal force pulled her down by her feet. The girl screamed and gasped, clinging to the marble rim of the bathtub. Her nails broke and she was dragged into the water. She kicked and flailed her arms, but the little girl who was dragging her towards the bottom of the tub looked at her face and Lizzy understood in that instant that she had no more hope. She felt a grip on her neck, the shower hose had wrapped around her neck. She ran out of breath and stopped moving. She died in silence and nobody noticed.

06

The Kitchen

Rooney was wearing a pajama set made up of a white and blue striped half-sleeved shirt and a light blue shorts. He had two mismatched black slippers on his feet. He came out of the room, scratched his rough butt, and then opened the main door.

"Has it always been like this?" he wondered.

The staircase in front of him, instead of going down, was going up. The boy was starving, despite having eaten all that junk food, he wanted something more substantial. He began to climb the stairs, did a first staircase of thirty steps and due to exhaustion decided to sit and rest.

"Where are you, damn kitchen?" he said out of breath.

Rooney noticed that the pictures on the brown walls were all crooked. There was not one straight, some were hanging to the right and others to the left. Even one was upside down.

"The old host?" said Rooney recognizing the man. He was in a photo with his family. In the other pictures there were photos of the locals, all in black and white.

In that moment, out of nowhere, a small chimpanzee appeared and took the black and white photo frame and destroyed it into a thousand pieces with sharp teeth that came out of his mouth. Rooney, out of great fear, began to run up the stairs, the monkey chased him with scary cries. The animal was small and cunning, it was black in color and had great strength.

Rooney reached a fuchsia door, opened it and closed it in the monkey's face. The boy found himself in an immense kitchen, there were two ovens, two sinks and three cooktops placed at an angle on the front and right walls. Everything was in steel and well taken care of, in the center of the room there was a round table with a chair. On a red tablecloth was placed a roasted chicken with potatoes that Rooney was captivated by. Red wine was poured into a crystal glass to accompany the dish. The forks were silver, the knives gold. The walls of the room were ivory white, there were no windows, and a four-meter-wide refrigerator was placed on the left wall. A chandelier with four light bulbs illuminated the entire room.

"What goodness!" said Rooney with great surprise.

Without even thinking twice, he sat down to eat the chicken, bit into it with great fervor, and drank the wine.

"Baam", the monkey knocked down the door and Rooney trembled with fear. As soon as he crossed the threshold, the door behind the monkey disappeared and became a wall. Rooney had no way out, he opened a kitchen drawer and took a long and sharp knife with a black handle.

"Come on monkey! Were you spying on me, weren't you? I saw you among the trees!" said Rooney.

"Grr Grr" the monkey screamed and her eyes lit up green.

Rooney was very scared, his heart was racing. The monkey jumped on the table, the boy started to circle around it. The beast looked at him with angry eyes and opened its teeth, ready to bite. Rooney grabbed a ladle and threw it at it. The chimpanzee destroyed it with its teeth. The room grew in size, the walls moved away further and further. Rooney found himself alone next to the refrigerator, the monkey was more than ten meters away. Rooney opened the fridge and saw some bananas. He took them and the monkey started to smell the scent in the air. The boy threw the bananas in various directions to distract the animal. The monkey went left and he went right.

"I have to find an exit! Cursed house let me out!" he cursed.

The boy started to beat his hands against the wall with great desperation, the chimpanzee had already eaten two bananas and only two remained. The kitchen's morphology was all altered, the table was gone, the fridge had shrunk. At that moment, the two large ovens lit up and scorching flames appeared inside. Rooney took other knives from the drawers and pots.

"Uah! Uah! Uah!" the monkey screamed.

It grew in size, it became one meter and seventy. It had a menacing and angry look, Rooney was afraid. He had never felt such a sharp pain in his chest before this misadventure.

"Let's get it over with, ugly monkey! I'll eat you!" Rooney yelled.

"Wraaaa!" the chimpanzee replied.

The monkey ran towards him and Rooney threw the pots at it, but he didn't hit it. When it reached the boy, the animal jumped and opened its teeth. Skillfully, Rooney inserted a knife between its jaws and escaped. The monkey screamed in pain, it had been wounded. The knife had perforated its palate. He took it out of his mouth and lost a lot of blood. Nonetheless, he chased after Rooney who was heading for the ovens. The boy opened one, it was large and had an arched opening. The flames were blinding, the temperature reached 3000 degrees Celsius.

"Come on, monkey! Come take the banana!" said Rooney showing it to her.

The monkey fell for it and took the banana with its teeth. Rooney grabbed it by the neck with great force, threw it in the oven, and locked it inside.

"Uraaah!" the monkey screamed in pain. It melted like ice in the sun.

At that moment, the room started to spin around.

"Let's play, let's play, monkey!" said the little girl who appeared out of nowhere.

"Who are you?" asked Rooney, not understanding anything.

"What did you do to my monkey?" the girl asked.

"Uh, uh..." Rooney couldn't speak.

The girl, realizing that the monkey had been burned alive, grew taller than Rooney, her eyes bled, and she grabbed the boy by the throat with immense strength and threw him into the second oven.

"Help! Help me! Jooohn! Let me out!" the boy cried out in vain.

The girl turned on the oven and the flames enveloped him. Rooney screamed in vain, the girl was pleased and laughed with joy. Her game had just begun.

07

The Love

John was playing and joking with Janine, when suddenly he heard Rooney's scream. At the same time, it seemed distant and close.

"What are you thinking?" Janine said, giving him a slap on the forehead and making him come to his senses.

"You'll pay for this!" John said, Janine ran away and the boy chased her again.

The house changed shape again without the two of them realizing it. They entered a room with walls half green and half black. Janine stopped suddenly.

"What's happening?" John asked.

"Look at this basket" Janine replied.

"Dolls?" John said.

It was a basket full of dolls and stuffed animals. Nude or dressed, but they had something special.

"This one doesn't have eyes and this one doesn't have ears" John noticed.

"This one doesn't have hair and these two others don't have a body" Janine noted.

"Look here, it has an eye that pops out of the socket" Janine whispered, holding the doll out to John.

John felt a chill down his back as if someone was watching them. He realized he shouldn't touch those dolls, someone wouldn't like it.

"We have to leave immediately!" John yelled.

"Come on, wait, let me see this other one" Janine said.

John took the girl by the hand and brought her out of the room with force. Then he closed the door.

"What's wrong with you? Why are you acting like this?" Janine said, frightened, and ran away crying.

"Janine, stop!" John said, trying in vain to grab her.

Meanwhile, Robin had entered Barbara's room. He approached her quietly and hugged her from behind.

"Aaah!" Barbara cried out, turning around with a frightened look.

"What a face you made!" Robin laughed.

"You're a fool!" said Barbara and pushed him away.

"It was just a joke, I wanted to keep you company" said Robin with a warm gaze.

"Okay, fool" said Barbara and then kissed him.

After kissing, the two lay in bed. They looked into each other's eyes and laughed. They bit each other and kissed. Robin took off his shirt.

"What are you doing? Have you gone crazy?" Barbara cried out, blushing with embarrassment.

"Don't you want to?" asked Robin.

"Of course, I do" Barbara replied and kissed him passionately.

Suddenly, there was a vibrating noise.

"Let's play! Come on, let's play!" said the girl in her thin voice.

The two were frightened.

"Where did she come from?" asked Barbara.

"I didn't see her come in" Robin replied.

The girl appeared out of nowhere, running back and forth and throwing everything she could find. Food, nail polish, perfumes, clothes. Then she jumped on the bed several times and Robin grabbed her by the arm.

"Now you stay quiet and good here inside!" said Robin and locked her in a room with a key.

"Let me out!" the girl shouted while pounding on the door.

"What have you done! Are you sure we can do this? I'm scared" Barbara asked, embracing Robin tightly out of fear.

"I have no idea who she is and where she came from" Robin replied, frightened.

The girl smiled and blood flowed from her eyes. On the shelf above the heads of the two young people was a statue of a black, shiny elephant. The girl seemed to call it to her with a gesture, and the artifact fell from above, right on top of Robin's head. The boy didn't even have time to realize what was happening and fell off the bed. The impact was heavy. Part of his skull was damaged and a river of blood was pouring out of his head. He couldn't breathe or talk well, his eyes pleaded for help. He began to have an epileptic seizure, the tonic-clonic contractions were impressive.

"No!" Barbara screamed so loudly that John and Janine heard her from a distance.

"Stop Janine!" John shouted and grabbed her by the hand.

"It's Barbara! We have to go to her!" Janine understood.

The two kids found themselves in a narrow hallway with black walls, with paintings of strange spirals that disturbed the kids.

"Where are we?" Janine asked.

"I don't know, I don't remember being in this place" John replied.

At the end of the hallway, they reached a red door and opened it. They saw Robin's lifeless body and Barbara crying. John threw himself on his friend's body and cried bitterly.

"What happened? How is this possible? Robin, respond!" John called in vain.

As soon as those words were spoken, the girl passed through the door.

"Let's plaaaay!" she cried with a ghostly voice.

"It's a ghost! Help!" Barbara screamed.

In an instant, the girl entered Barbara's body. The girl changed appearance, became thin, tall, with white hair and wrinkled hands. She had long claws and stinky saliva dripped from her mouth. The skin was dry and gray. John was terrified by her bloodshot eyes. Barbara was no longer in control.

"Let's run!" John said, took the elephant statue and ran away with Janine.

They ran as fast as they could, passed under a marble arch, turned right and then left. They arrived at a spiral staircase, went down without looking back, and finally found themselves in a barn full of chickens and hay bales.

"How did we end up here?" Janine asked.

"I don't know, this place is cursed! Our friends have been killed, who knows how Rooney and Lizzy are doing. I have a bad feeling" John said with fear.

The barn was all red and the chickens filled most of it. They roamed free and ate the grain on the ground. There was a wooden ladder that led to the upper floor, which was open halfway. From the top, you could see the chickens and the rest of the barn. There were no exit doors and the ladder from where they came disappeared suddenly.

"Bruum" a loud noise was heard.

"Ghà ghà ghà! Let's play friends!" Barbara shouted aboard a green tractor.

The monster that appeared in front of them did not resemble their friend at all.

"Get on Janine, I'll distract her!" John said and the girl nodded.

John held the elephant in his hands and the ghost aimed at him. The boy understood the situation and tried to use it to his advantage. The monster was chasing him aboard the tractor and John was running through the chickens. He stood in front of the hay bales and started shouting: "You want the elephant! Come and get it!"

The tractor went at full speed, the ghost reached out with his hand from the vehicle. With his claws, he attacked John. The boy escaped at the last minute and the ghost fell from the tractor that crashed into the hay bales. Taking advantage of the daze, John used the elephant to break the ghost's skull.

In that moment, the statue shattered into a thousand pieces and the ghost left Barbara's dead body. Janine's tears were sad and bitter, but she knew that nothing could save her anymore. The girl ran down and rejoined John. The young man hugged her and as he looked into her eyes, a chasm opened beneath them. The two young people fell into a basement.

08

The Flower

Are you okay?" John asked, offering his hand to help Janine get up.

"Yes, it's really cold down here" the girl said, hugging herself.

Suddenly, someone approached stealthily. "It's all your fault! His anger will never stop!"

John and Janine hesitated for a moment.

"You bastard! You tricked us!" John shouted and grabbed him by the throat. "You brought us to a cursed place!"

"Mercy! Mercy on me!" the old owner implored.

"Let him go" Janine intervened, and the boy loosened his grip.

The old man coughed and sat down in a brown, old and worn-out armchair. The two young people looked around and realized that they were in a bad and cramped place, full of mold, cobwebs, and rats. The walls were gray and rotten, there was a broken bed and a small table with tools like a hammer and a saw. Some candles were scattered here and there to light the basement.

"What is this place?" John asked.

"It's my camp. I live here" the old man replied.

"In here? Why?" Janine asked.

"This house has been cursed, it's no longer mine" Edgar replied.

"Then why do you live here? Why didn't you run away? We wouldn't have met you if you weren't here!" John said with uncontrollable anger.

"I can't abandon this house. No one can. Not even the residents of Marcoons can abandon this mountain" the old man replied.

"Speak old man! I'm tired of your lies!" John threatened, brandishing a hammer.

"Alright" the old man coughed with a wicked laugh. "I can't die, but you can! She always wants new souls to feed on!"

"Who is she?" Janine asked.

"Her name is Margaret. She's Judith's sister, the innkeeper's daughter" the old man replied.

John was shocked, then he thought about those words and realized that the two girls looked very similar. They had braids and similar dresses, only their eyes and hair color changed. She was the one he had seen before on the rocking chair. When he left the tavern, he noticed the sadness of the young girl who had served him buffalo meat with great joy.

"How is this possible? Are you all ghosts?" John asked.

"We are between life and death. We belong to her, she can do what she wants. I've lived on this mountain since 1880" the old man replied.

"For all these years, have you brought children to this house?" Janine asked.

"Anyone who wanted to follow me, men, women, or children" the old man replied.

"You dirty son of a bitch!" John shouted and hit him in the face with a punch. The man laughed and spat blood.

"I can't die, you can do whatever you want. It won't change anything" the old man laughed wickedly.

"Who transformed that girl into this monstrous creature?" Janine asked.

"An ancient, very dark magic, summoned by the girl herself, because of me" Edgar replied regretfully.

"What are you talking about? What did you do to her?" Janine asked with a bitter face.

The old man shuddered. "My son Luis was a boy with a heart of gold. He loved that girl more than his life. She was beautiful, she looked like an angel. She often came to play in this house. Dark thoughts clouded my mind, I gave everything I had to divert my attention from these thoughts. But I couldn't. One time I asked her to help me bring some packages to the basement. I locked the door and with force I raped her sexually on this table" the old man said regretfully.

John grabbed him by the neck and squeezed as hard as he could. "You're a coward! How could you do this to her? Your death will be slow and painful! You will be damned forever!"

"I already know that" the old man said with short breath. "I can't die, let me go. I know how to defeat her!"

John reluctantly let him go.

"Tell us what we have to do!" shouted Janine.

The old man coughed, then spoke: "During the act, the girl was agitated. She was about to run away and so I strangled her. Before she breathed her last breath, she spoke strange words. I didn't understand their meaning, but she cursed the house and all the town's inhabitants, even a monkey and a small toy elephant that became stone and have haunted the house for decades. They are her servants."

"That cursed elephant I destroyed with my own hands! Two of my friends have died because of this ghost and I don't know if the others are okay. Tell me exactly what words she spoke!" cursed John.

"Arumath, Aruntur, Arutha" replied the old man.

"Goddess Arumath, destroy their lives for me" translated John.

"Do you know this language?" asked Janine.

"Yes, it's an ancient magic language used by Wiccan witches. Arumath is an ancient Egyptian goddess, protector of young girls. Many young women honored her with offerings to receive protection from all evil. The girl invoked the goddess out of desperation and she took possession of her soul. I don't know from which dark book she studied these words, perhaps from the Black Grimoire of Satan. I think she only spoke them out of fear, she certainly didn't know what she was doing" explained John.

"Exactly, boy! I noticed that there was a symbol like an A engraved on her skin! I've read that cursed book of hers. I am chained in this place and I cannot leave the house for more than half a day. However, in these years I have discovered how to defeat her! The only solution to end the curse is to create a circle of white flowers around the house" said the owner.

"Now I understand why there are all those flowers. There's an empty spot! Why is there a missing flower?" asked John.

"The last flower must be a Leontopodium Alpinum and must be planted in that precise spot by a young man with a pure heart who knows how to love his sweetheart!" explained the old man.

John looked at Janine in amazement. "An Alpine Starflower? But that's a flower that grows in Europe, it's impossible to find it around here!"

The old man took a tile from the floor and pulled out that very flower inside a vase. It was white and looked like a star, had few green leaves, a short stem, and the flower heads resembling a lion's paw.

"My son's eyes point to that precise spot where you will plant it!" shouted the old man.

"Do those skulls belong to your family?" asked Janine.

"Yes, the curse took away everything that was most dear to me. My fourteen-year-old son Luis, my eight-year-old daughter Gwen, and my wife Jane. They died at the will of the goddess, they were the first souls she devoured. Their bodies turned to bones instantly. At the time I was thirty-five," explained the old man. He placed the white flower on a worn-out table.

Janine turned away from the old man, looked into John's eyes and took his hands affectionately.

"Together we can make it! We'll escape from here!" comforted Janine. At that very moment, the old owner started to cry blood, grasped a sharp knife and stabbed Janine in the back. The weapon came out of her chest and the girl spat blood.

"No! Janineee!" John cried out in vain, the girl's body collapsed to the ground without strength.

The old man's head rotated 360 degrees and then exploded into a thousand pieces. John tried to stop the bleeding with his hands, but the blood wouldn't stop.

"It's going to be okay Janine, I'll be able to save you. Hold on!" said John desperately.

Janine smiled. "I...I...will l-l-ove you f-f-orever" she stammered.

With tears in his eyes, John kissed the girl. It lasted for an instant, but for them it was a moment of true love. Janine stopped breathing, her eyes went out with sadness. John cried and shouted to the sky.

"L-l-let's play John!" said Janine with a shrill voice. There was an evil grin on her face and her blood-filled wicked eyes stared at John with anger.

"Janine? No! You're Margaret! Cursed!" shouted John and he quickly backed away from the girl.

Janine had been possessed by the ghost; she got up from the ground and took the knife out of her back. She gripped it and threatened John.

"You're the only one left! Arumath's revenge is about to be fulfilled!" Janine shouted with a ghostly and icy voice.

"Wake up Janine! You must stop!" shouted John.

John tore the flower from the vase and started running. He passed through a door and found himself in a dark place. It felt like being in a black vortex, the boy ran in the dark without seeing anything. At a certain point, he arrived in a well-lit room, there were strange symbols drawn on the walls in blue, red, and green colors.

"The Symbol of Arumath!" John realized.

The boy opened a door and found himself facing a wall with only one hole at the bottom. He had to crawl through it to escape the ghost. The monster's screams were getting closer and closer. John crawled into that gap and arrived in an underground tunnel. At some point he fell into the void and found himself in the pink-walled room. On a white sofa in front of him was Janine.

"Come to me, John. We'll stay together forever!" said the ghost with open arms.

"How could you do this to me? You destroyed everything I had!" John exclaimed.

"I lost everything! My life was taken and now I'll take it from all of you!" Janine shouted, showing her long teeth and eyes full of blood and anger.

John was in panic, he didn't know what to do. Suddenly he felt a heat envelop him, a white and pure energy passed behind him and then flew towards the ceiling.

"Guys, is that you?" John said, shocked. In that white energy he saw the faces of his friends, with their strength they made the glass chandelier fall on top of the ghost's head. The being screamed and was blocked for a moment, his friends attacked the house and created a gap to the outside. John ran away without turning back, he saw the skulls and the smaller one showed him the right way to reach the empty place in the circle. John rushed full of courage, he was almost able to reach the exact spot when an immense force knocked him to the ground.

"Graaaah!" the ghost shouted. With enormous jaws, it bit into the boy's right leg. Janine's body could no longer stand and was crawling on the ground.

John, despite the pain, also crawled to reach the exact spot. He stretched out his arm and planted the Alpine Star he had kept in the palm of his hand right in that precise spot. The white flowers lit up in unison, the ghost screamed in pain and was forced to abandon Janine's body.

"Dammit! How dare you! I am Arumath!" the goddess shouted.

The house crumbled into itself, shattered into a thousand pieces, and then turned to dust. The symbol of Arumath disappeared, the city of Marcoons vanished along with all its inhabitants. Everyone laughed and felt finally free. The souls of the dead that had been absorbed by Arumath over the years emerged from her essence. The goddess exploded and emitted a light so bright it was visible across all the United States.

"Alpine Star is your favorite flower, Mom. It grows in arid places, on mountains, and withstands anything. It's not afraid of anything, just like you" John said through tears.

John had received a fatal wound. He smiled with his gaze turned towards the sky.

"The House of Death no longer existed, it is said that on that day, someone saw children holding hands ascend to heaven on a white ladder. At the end of the line, two twin girls held hands and laughed along with the others".

THE END

Acknowledgments

Thank you for making it this far. Below you can read my experience that inspired me to write this novel, taken from my book "The Dreams of My Mind".

The Ghost - Between Dream and Reality

This story that I'm about to tell you is at the limit between dream and reality. It happened when I was 10 years old, during the Christmas period between December 24th and 26th, in Morcone, in the province of Benevento. We were three families for a total of ten people, we quickly reached the small mountain town. I remember it had many houses, all close to each other, but ours was more isolated. The roads and streets in the town were very steep, there were few shops and a church. The house we had rented for the Christmas period was big and had ten rooms, two dining rooms, each with a fireplace. There was also a small garden attached with small trees and acorns scattered on the ground. I, my sister, and a friend of mine went exploring. Under the house was a large parking lot, narrow, cold and ghostly. Inside we found a basket full of toys, they were all broken. There were many dolls without heads or eyes. The two girls wanted to take them, but I said no. I felt a strange presence, something that made me understand that those dolls belonged to someone and we should not touch them.

In general, the days were happy and fun, but some mysteries remain unsolved. In the evenings, strange noises were always heard, the paintings hanging on the walls, at night were straight and the next morning they were crooked. We always put them back in the straight position, but the next day they were crooked again. Maybe the cause was the slope of the house. This was noticed by everyone.

One night it was cold, I had to go to the bathroom. I took courage and went. I went back to bed and after a little while I heard that in one room they were complaining of the cold because someone had opened the window. Suddenly, the window in front of me opened and the shutter went down and went up by itself. I thought it was a dream, I put my head under the covers and prayed. Everything quieted down and I fell asleep.

The next day I didn't say anything, I played as usual for the house. I took a scooter that was in one dining room and with it I traveled the long hallway that led from one dining room to the other. Along the sides of the hallway were several rooms. While I was going back and forth at great speed, I noticed in a room on the left a black rocking chair and on it a girl. I thought it was my sister, but I decided not to stop and continue to the dining room and then come back and go in that room and play with the rocking chair. When I got to the dining room, I found my sister, so I was very surprised. Who was that girl on the rocking chair? So, I went in that room and there was no one, I played a little on the rocking chair and then I went away. Time later, thinking about her appearance, I can say she had a black dress in the late 1800s style, black hair, and a white face that I don't remember the features of. Strange thing about that house was that the owner, when he came to say hello, never wanted to come in, he always stayed at the entrance and always said that the house was for sale.

Months after that vacation, we got together with the other two families to spend time together. My mother had made a home movie with the camera, three copies, one for each family. Today, for some strange reason that I ignore, these three tapes have disappeared. All three were lost and no one knows the reason. I saw the tape twice, it was very funny and there was nothing unusual. During the reunion, someone said that the house was haunted by ghosts. At that age, I was only ten years old, I didn't know what ghosts were. A distant aunt said she had seen an old woman on the rocking chair, while my friend said she had seen a little girl. I said nothing. I don't know if they were lying or if what I had seen was just a dream or pure reality.

Printed in Great Britain
by Amazon

18226363R00048